KINDA BLUE

by Ann Grifalconi

One day down in Georgia,
Where the sweet corn grows so slow,
I had me a fit of lonely.
I was feelin' kinda blue.

Little, Brown and Company
Boston Toronto London

For all the family love in the world

First Edition

Library of Congress Cataloging-in-Publication Data

Grifalconi, Ann.
Kinda blue / by Ann Grifalconi. — 1st ed
p. cm.
Summary: Sissy feels lonely and blue until her uncle Dan cheers her up by explaining that everything, even corn, needs special attention every now and then.
ISBN 0-316-32869-3
[1. Uncles — Fiction. 2. Afro-Americans — Fiction.] I. Title.
PZ7.G8813Ki 1993
[E] — dc20 92-1399

0 9 8 7 6 5 4 3 2 1

NIL

Published simultaneously in Canada
by Little, Brown & Company (Canada) Limited

Paintings done in watercolor, pastel, and colored pencil on watercolor paper.
Text set in Palatino by United Lithograph.
Color separations made by New Interlitho.
Printed and bound by New Interlitho.
Printed in Italy

Yes, one day down in Georgia,
Feelin' kinda low,
Had an awful fit of lonely,
And I didn't know what to do.

There I was, settin' all by myself
Scrooched down in the front yard
Of our Georgia farm,
Pokin' holes in the dirt for no good reason.
Me and my bent-over shadow —
Blue!

Now, it didn't matter to me
That Mama and Gran'ma was up to the house,
And it didn't matter
That I was just short of seven.
It didn't matter to me:
I was seized by that fit of lonely,
And I didn't care who knew!

I guess it all got started
'Cause I got to missin' my papa.
(He had died back when I was a baby girl.)
It didn't seem fair.
"Other kids got papas!" I sniffed.
I was feeling awful sorry for myself.

I looked around, all grumpy-like.
"Nobody ever be there when you need 'em!"
Brother, sister — always playin' somewhere else.
Mama, Gran'ma — always busy, busy.
Gran'pa always settin' on his porch.
Uncle Dan always in his ol' cornfields.

"What you doin' over there, Sissy Honey?"
This-here cheerful voice called out.
"Scratchin' in ground like ol' wet hen?"

I knowed it was just Uncle Dan,
So I kept on diggin', mumblin',
"I'm gonna dig me a hole s-o-o deep . . ."

"What's that you say?"
Uncle said, comin' closer.

I said it louder:
"I said I'm gonna dig me a hole s-o-o deep,
I can climb right in and hide!"
'Course, it came out real grumpy-like,
'N' Uncle was having none of that!

So he bent his big tall frame
And scooped me right up!
He knowed I loved to be carried
Up on his shoulders, so high.
"How 'bout takin' a ride with me, Sissy?
I'm goin' to visit my corn children!"

I shook my head, my mouth tight shut,
Still holdin' on to my grumpy.
"Cat got your tongue?"
Uncle smiled, catchin' on.
But he kept walkin'.
Holdin' me steady with his strong right arm,
He went right 'cross the road to his fields of corn,
Growin' straight and shy and bright
'Neath the shade of Ol' Sadie Mountain.

"See them fling they leafy arms?"
Uncle said. "They wavin' hello!"

The tall cornstalks did look
Like rows of dancers,
Silky white heads tossin' in the sunlight.

And Uncle Dan commenced to wave
Right back at them!
(Looked so silly — made me giggle.)

Then Uncle played right back to me.
"Don't laugh! They talks to me!"

"Oh, Uncle, hush! No such thing!
Just cornstalks, rustlin' in the breeze!"

Uncle laughed.
"Cat don't got your tongue no more!"

Then he pointed proudly back to his corn children.
"I raised 'em from seed, I did.
Watched over 'em.
Why, I bet I knows every one of 'em!"

"Every one?
Oh, Uncle, that couldn't be.
They all 'xactly the same!"

Uncle Dan slid a sly look at me.
"So you thinks they all be the same?
Let's play us a game 'n' find out."

Settin' me down on the old fence rail
That snaked around his field,
Uncle Dan, in one long, swingin' stride,
Reached one of the tall cornstalks,
Pulled off an ear of corn,
And handed it back to me,
Still wrapped in its green husk,
Sayin', "Peel it open!"
Which be what I did,
'Til the little rows of golden corn shone free.

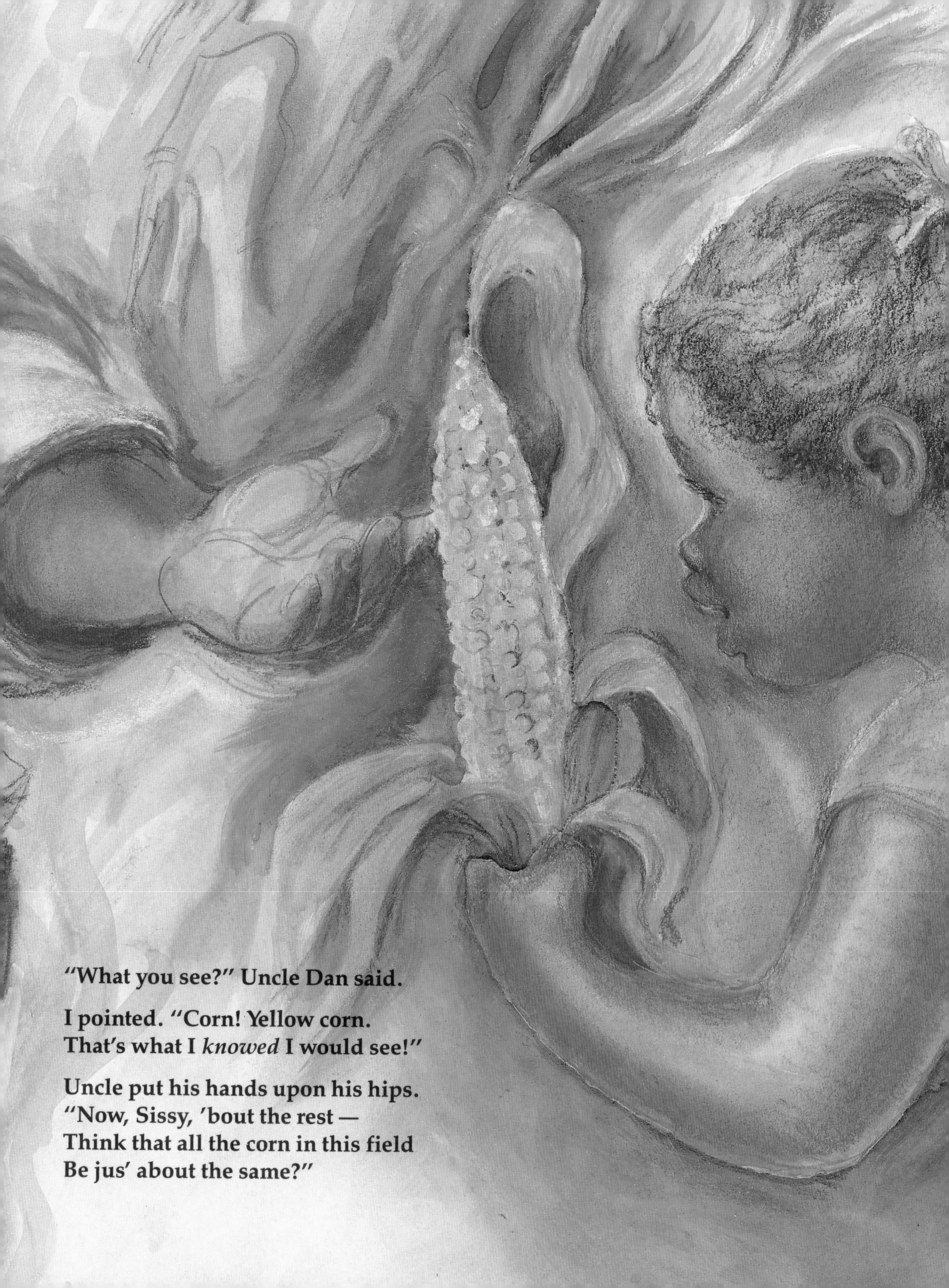

"What you see?" Uncle Dan said.

I pointed. "Corn! Yellow corn.
That's what I *knowed* I would see!"

Uncle put his hands upon his hips.
"Now, Sissy, 'bout the rest —
Think that all the corn in this field
Be jus' about the same?"

"Well, Uncle," I said, careful-like,
"Let's stick to the ears of corn."
Uncle nodded. (He saw I was sharp!)
I took my time. "Maybe not all the ears
Be the same size . . .
Or just as ripe . . .
But one thing for sure,
They all be yellow!"
(I knowed what color corn was —
I ate it all the time!)

Uncle Dan bared his teeth in a foxy grin.
"That so?" he said.
Then he pointed.
"Now, see that pretty one over there?
Just go on over
'N' pick yourself one sweet little corn ear, Sissy!"
And he lifted me down to the ground.
"Hurry on, now!"

But 'cause I was still
Kinda blue around the edges,
I didn't hurry, not me!
I walked over lazy-like
To pull one off, re-al easy —
To show that I was cool.
(But with my hands
Half the size of Uncle's,
It was tough to break one from the stalk!)

But I got me an ear
And held it high to show it off!

Uncle told me, "Open it!"
And then he said, "Look again!"

And then I saw something very strange.

Some of the kernels was *red*
And some, *blue!*

I still had my mouth open when Uncle said,
"Now you think they all be the same?"

I shook my head.
"Not me, Uncle!"

Uncle Dan smiled. "See now?
Every one's different."

"Just the way we be?" I asked.

Uncle nodded and took me by the hand.
"Let's take a little get-acquainted walk."
We walked between the gangly cornstalks,
Their leafy arms patting us, friendly-like,
As if to say hello.

Made me feel a little better, somehow.

"Uncle," I said then, "do plants feel?
Could they feel sad
The way we does?"

"Kinda blue?" Uncle smiled and squeezed my hand.
"Why, sure, Sissy, sure they does!"

"How you tell?" I joked.
"They talks to you?"

Uncle laughed. "Well, they shows me. They really does!
They gives me signs."
He pointed to a nearby stalk.
"See? This one be drooping.
You touch a leaf —
Gone be limp, sure!"

Now I laughed — didn't he know?
"It just needs water, Uncle! Cain't you see?"

Uncle laughed and touched the top of my head.
"You're right. But now, ain't that jus' like us?
Sometimes we needs waterin', too!
We needs somebody to pay 'tention to us —
Water us when we be sad!"

He crouched down to look at me.
"Now, if you knows someone really well
And you looks *very* close,
You can always tell if they be happy or sad!"

"So, even when you thinks nobody cares,
Even when you wishes you had your own papa
To watch over you and take care of you . . ."

I looked up at him. How did he know?
He shook his head.
"Never you mind!
We *be* there, takin' care!"

"For why? Why would you care?" I asked.

"'Cause we loves you — for always —
No matter what. We all be family here."
I reached up and hugged him tight.

And that's when I let go some big tears
I had bottled up inside me.
And that bottle was tilting
And pouring out all my bad feelings
'Til I felt good all over.

Then Uncle Dan hugged me back
And carried me all the way home.
And I knew
There was no way
I would ever feel as blue or as lonely
Again.